D0992139

THE TALE OF TUPPENNY

Beatrix Potter

THE TALE OF TUPPENNY

Illustrated by Marie Angel

FREDERICK WARNE

FREDERICK WARNE

Penguin Books Ltd, Harmondsworth, Middlesex, England
Viking Penguin Inc., 40 West 23rd Street, New York, New York 10010, U.S.A.
Penguin Books Australia Ltd, Ringwood, Victoria, Australia
Penguin Books Canada Ltd, 2801 John Street, Markham, Ontario, Canada L3R 1B4
Penguin Books (N.Z.) Ltd, 182–190 Wairau Road, Auckland 10, New Zealand

First published 1973
Reprinted 1976 and 1980
This edition 1985
The text of this story is taken from
A History of the Writings of Beatrix Potter, F. Warne & Co.
Text copyright © Frederick Warne & Co., 1971
Illustrations copyright © Marie Angel, 1973

ISBN 0 7232 1724 6

Printed and bound in Great Britain by
William Clowes Limited, Beccles and London

IN the land of Green Ginger there is a town called Marmalade, which is exclusively inhabited by guinea-pigs.

They are of all colours, and of two sorts—the common ordinary smooth-haired guinea-pigs who run errands and keep greengrocers shops—and the kind that call themselves Abyssinian Cavies—who wear ringlets and walk upon their toes.

And the short-haired guinea-pigs admire and envy the curls of the long-haired guinea-pigs.

Both kinds of guinea-pigs go to the Barber especially on Saturdays.

The Barber brushes and combs and curls the top-knots of the Abyssinian Cavies, and trims their whiskers, but he cannot do very much for the smooth-haired guinea-pigs – except apply pomatum – which has no effect, only making their smooth hair even flatter than it was before.

Now this Barber was an ingenious person, he invented a new hair-wash in the back shops. I do not know what it was made of (which is perhaps well).

He called it Quintessence of Abyssinian Artichokes, and drew up an untruthful advertisement, to the effect that it would cause asparagus to grow upon a doorknob—and bushy hair upon the tails of rats (which is said to be really the case amongst the Pyrenees!).

11

Then he put the advertisement, and 6 large bottles of the new essence, in the shop window.

There was immediately a crowd of short-haired guinea-pigs.

The barber's little guinea-pig son came out and distributed hand-bills which stated that the Quintessence of Abyssinia was an infallible cure for chicken-pox.

The Abyssinian Cavies were disgusted.

The smooth-haired guinea-pigs came daily and flattened their noses against the barber's window; but they hesitated to buy; because one bottle cost 8 pepper-corns–(or post-free for half a potato)–and also because the long-haired guinea-pigs had spread an insidious and libellous report that the hair-wash was made of slugs.

The short-haired guinea-pigs discussed the matter at street corners–but no one would try the first bottleful!

Now it happened that in that town there was a guinea-pig called Tuppenny, who was a miserable object, because most of his hair had been pulled out—

(I do not know what for, but I have no doubt that he deserved it.)

The friends of Tuppenny were sorry for him and condoled with him; and told him that he was not fit to be seen, and they offered to subscribe for a bottle of the new Quint-essence.

Tuppenny himself had become indifferent to appearances; but he was over-persuaded by the sympathetic affection of his friends, and permitted himself to be led away.

At the Barber's, the friends produced 8 peppercorns, and the Barber applied the hair-wash with a garden syringe, in order–(as he explained)–not to wet his own hands with it. He said that the prescription was very powerful.

It had a peculiar smell which immediately excited the attention of Mrs. Tuppenny, when her husband returned home. His friends accompanied him as far as his door.

Tuppenny passed a disturbed night, but looked much as usual in the morning. His hair had *not* grown.

His friends again conducted him to the Barber's and expostulated. The Barber was perplexed. After some argument he agreed to supply a second bottle at half-price. Tuppenny's head felt very hot during the night. But his hair was not any longer the next morning!

All the short-haired guinea-pigs in Marmalade were indignant. They demanded a third bottle of hair-wash free–gratis–for nothing at all.

The Barber was seriously alarmed, and remonstrated; he said that the stuff was so powerful that an over-dose might turn Tuppenny blue or even make him grow a tail.

But the friends carried their point.

There was quite a crowd of smooth-haired guinea-pigs in Tuppenny's front garden next morning–until Mrs. Tuppenny came out with a mop.

Tuppenny himself stayed late in bed. And when he did appear he looked very odd: his hair was certainly growing, especially on his nose.

His friends conducted him in triumph to the Barber's; his hair grew another inch while on the way; and when he reached the shop it was all over his ears, and he was surrounded by a twittering crowd of short-haired guinea-pigs.

The Barber received them with jubilation and raised the price per bottle to 20 pepper-corns.

There was no immediate sale however. The other guinea-pigs decided to wait a few days, to see whether Tuppenny's hair might change colour – or fall off!

Tuppenny would have been thankful! had it done so! The way that guinea-pig's hair grew was perfectly frightful!

The family couldn't bear him! and when he went out the rude little guinea-pig boys ran after him shouting 'old whiskers!!'

He went to the Barber's every morning to have it cut; but it grew again before he got home.

When he had spent all his money upon shaving, his family cut it themselves with scissors, all crooked and jagged behind, and stuffed pincushions with the snippings.

As for the Barber–his shop was deserted, and after a time he put up his shutters and ran away.

Then the rats took possession.

They ate up all the pomade and drank up all the remaining bottles of the celebrated hair-wash; but it had no effect upon them (they being bailiffs).

– And what has become of Tuppenny?

He has sold himself to a travelling show-man; who goes about the country with a tent; and a brass band; and a menagerie of five Polecats and Weasels; and a troupe of performing fleas; and the Fat Dormouse of Salisbury; and

TUPPENNY the HAIRY GUINEA-pig who lives in a caravan!

The End.